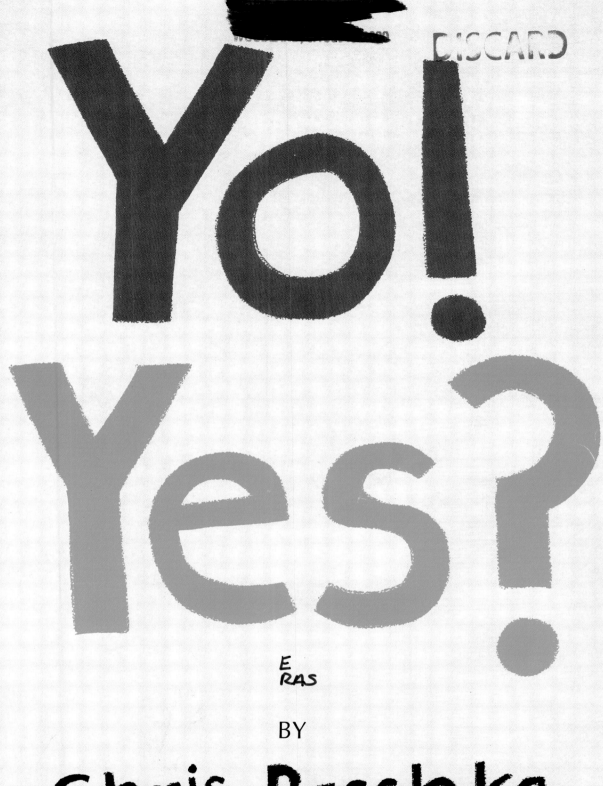

Yo! Yes?

BY

Chris Raschka

ORCHARD BOOKS NEW YORK

Orchard Books, 95 Madison Avenue, New York, NY 10016

Manufactured in the United States of America. Printed by Barton Press, Inc. Bound by Horowitz/Rae. Book design by Chris Raschka. The text of this book is hand lettered. The illustrations are watercolor and charcoal pencil, reproduced in full color.

Library of Congress Cataloging-in-Publication Data
Raschka, Christopher.
Yo! Yes? / Chris Raschka.   p.   cm. "A Richard Jackson book"—P.
Summary: Two lonely characters, one black and one white, meet on the street and become friends.
ISBN 0-531-05469-1.   ISBN 0-531-08619-4 (lib. bdg.)
[1. Friendship—Fiction.   2. Race relations—Fiction.   3. Afro-Americans—Fiction.]   I. Title.   PZ7.R18148Yo 1993
[E]—dc20   92-25644

FOR

my parents

Yes ?

Hey!

Who?

You!

Yes, you.

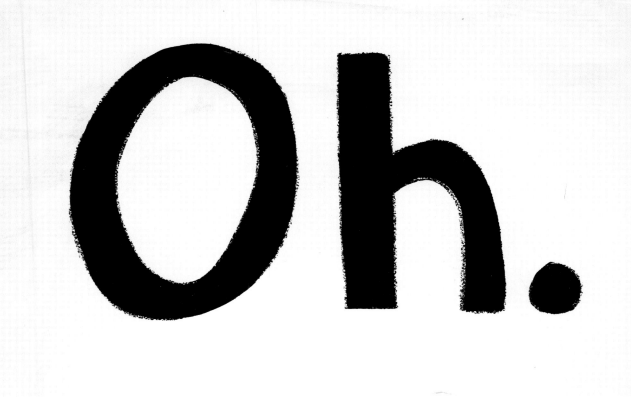

What's up?

Not much.

Why?

No fun.

Oh?

No
friends.

Oh!

Yes.

Look!

Hmmm?

Me!

You?

Yes, me!

You!

Well?

Well.

Yo!